OUR MAN

a novella

OUR MAN

a novella

Hal Hartley

ELBORO

OUR MAN

a novella

Published in New York by Elboro Press

ISBN: 978-1-7379274-4-0

First Edition, 2026 – Second Printing

Find more books by Hal Hartley and others at:
www.elboropress.com

For Hal Hartley's films and music, visit:
www.halhartley.com

OUR MAN

ONE

The issue of course is the girl. Seated at the bar, she is flanked by her parents, a well-off White couple probably a decade or so younger than our man. They adore their pretty and charming daughter who is, he guesses, anywhere from eighteen to twenty-five. He notices she's got a small bottle of expensive bubbly water before her while her parents are drinking red wine.

Abstemious or just too young to drink?

It's six o'clock in lower Manhattan on a Saturday in late November and the restaurant is practically empty. Our man, who will remain nameless for reasons he'll unwrap for you later, is at a small table opposite the bar, about twelve or thirteen feet away, having just completed his expensive, tasty, though not entirely satisfying dinner.

Once again, as the parents talk past her, over and

around her head of dark loose curls, addressing something of concern only to themselves, the girl raises her arms, places her hands behind her neck, arches her spine, and twists around from the waist to work out some real or imagined kink at the small of her back.

And she flashes him a glance.

This has been going on for about half an hour, this little stretch she performs, this figured yawn, to use a phrase of DeLillo's, which shows off the top of her provocative lace underwear and the excruciating beauty of her supple young waist. This is all for his benefit apparently and he is happy to indulge her. An exquisite woman-child like this ought to be allowed to show herself off without apology and he thinks her parents would agree. The mother, for instance, can't keep her hands off her, from time to time absently sliding her palm up under the girl's loose fitting short cut sweater to enjoy the delicious smoothness of her child's back. And our hero discovers he is actually jealous.

The parents, though clearly North American, are now speaking French, interested in a news item on the television above the bar. It being a kind of high-end French bistro, the television is always tuned to the City of Light. The girl excuses herself and slides off the stool, pauses, and stands looking around as if lost, allowing herself to be admired.

Our man obliges. He's a team player.

Her well-worn pair of corduroy jeans ride low on her hip, a four-inch swath of flat belly bare beneath the edge of her sweater, the delicate waistband of her pale green lace thong presented for view pretty much exclusively to announce that there is nothing between the cheeks of her ass and the soft, snug, caressing corduroy. Her gaze brushes over our hero to make sure he's still watching. He smiles reassuringly and nods his head towards the stairs leading to the restrooms. She sees, smiles appreciatively, and moves off.

He pushes aside his plate, sips his wine, and returns to the novel he's brought with him. He's rereading all of Henry Miller because he's decided, finally, to begin writing stories, to dedicate himself to the written word as a method of grappling with the world he moves through, and Miller's example intrigues him for a number of reasons. For one thing, he began writing fairly late, in his thirties. Our man, our hero, the protagonist of what follows, is fifty-three and has made motion pictures professionally for the last twenty-five years. For the most part it's work he likes and feels he's good at. But not unlike the meal he has just finished, it costs a great deal and is less than satisfying. His interests, he sometimes thinks, are not mainstream enough to excite popular or critical interest. But neither are they sufficiently challenging and, who knows, culturally relevant enough to be plausibly eligible for grants. Again: who knows. Allowing this persistent conundrum to bump him into freewheeling reverie he fixates on the edge of the page he has been reading and mentally chases something terribly important that has just skittered across the surface of his mind. What was that? An idea? No, a feeling, a useful analogy, a twitch, an apt metaphor. He's arrived late to the wrong party. His social set, his artistic peers, are down the street somewhere in a dive bar and he's doing his best in some much more well-heeled soirée to be polite and accommodating to strangers who suspect he's not what he seems to be at all. He's not fooling anyone but they're very polite. Even though they find him vaguely disgraceful, something about his smile, say, rattles their own estimation of themselves. His hosts are wavering between suspicion and pity, attraction and contempt. It's genuine interest and an easygoing camaraderie one moment and then, suddenly, they're keeping their distance and he's out on the sidewalk. He removes his glasses and massages his temples. How, exactly, did he get from reading Miller to here?

By now, though, the girl is back. The parents are getting ready to go. They put their coats on, exchange effusive goodbyes with the bartender in French and collect their bags. It seems they have been shopping at all the high-end Soho boutiques. The girl pulls on one of her finely woven gloves which, he notices, match her underwear. As her parents lead the way out, she dips down to collect one last petite shopping bag wedged in behind the bar's brass foot rail, placing her other glove on the red Naugahyde seat of her stool. Standing and turning, she flutters her ungloved hand in a kind of unaimed goodbye to the nearly empty restaurant and tumbles lightly out onto the sidewalk as she slides into her coat.

Our man looks at the forgotten glove on the stool and then back at the entrance, waiting for the beautiful creature to duck back in. Returning his glance to the glove, he lifts his gaze a fraction and catches the bartender, Raul, doing the same, looking, intrigued, from the forgotten glove to our man. And so our protagonist now stands and approaches the bar with his empty glass as Raul resumes his well-honed nonchalance and busies himself with some receipts.

"Another Cote du Rhone, please, Raul."

The bartender turns away to find the bottle while our subject lifts the girl's glove and considers its lightness, its softness, its cleanliness. The wine is poured and, though Raul is doing his best to appear disinterested, our man suspects this impeccably well-mannered and astute professional knows him as well as, if not better, then he knows himself. He comes here once a month or so with the Mistress, a spectacularly attractive retired fashion model. No one takes much notice of him, of course, some middle-aged guy who reads a lot. But it's hard to forget the Mistress. Restaurants like these, both he and Raul understand, are created in the hopes of attracting women like her. But here our man is now, all alone, with his mind so obviously on the behind of some innocent and precocious teenager.

The object of our study now reaches back to remove his wallet from the pocket of his neatly creased trousers. Finding one of his business cards, he places it with care inside the glove which he then lays on the bar.

"For the lost and found."

Raul nods skeptically and takes the glove, placing it in a drawer beneath the cash register as our man, our representative though worrisome mensch, returns to his table to read more Henry Miller.

It's *Tropic of Cancer* he's reading again today because it was the first book Miller wrote that was published. That was 1934. Henry was forty-three. Our man simply wants to compare strategy. These are the days, this the hunger, these the ideas, the observations of a man in the early nineteen-thirties consumed with worlds of feeling and actively trying to find a form to cast it all in. Our man loves the adventure of the whole thing. There is a sense of accomplishment, one suspects, from spending the days piling up words, phrases, sentences, paragraphs articulating the world as felt in one's own heart, mind and body.

But is that practical?

Of course not. Though what, in his life thus far, has been? He shivers with a sense of private, illicit reaction. Even Miller and his companions way back when are insisting on *The Last Book*, an end to literature. No more books! Frustrated and fired-up young people as can be found in any generation. It's always a revolution for youth, it seems. Literature has to die in order for literature to live. And so on. Movies too. Poetry, theater, painting. He recalls his own feverish stabs at immortality at twenty and would blush if he could, but can't. Another luxury he long ago foreswore. What the fuck, he finally decides, just shut up and play your guitar. That's Frank Zappa talking, of course, a musician, dead since 1993 but still buzzing around in our man's consciousness on a daily basis. Miller sometimes reminds him of Zappa, constitutionally incapable of toeing the line, the popularly accepted, rigorously promoted, mainstream, sure-to-be-a-hit line.

He looks up from the book, unsure whether he has been

reading or thinking out loud. He tends to do that too, talk to himself, mumbling quietly as he thinks. But Raul is not watching him. The elderly couple off to his left do not appear concerned, horrified, or outraged. So he suspects that, no, he has not been talking to himself out loud. He also sees there is no pretty teenager come to retrieve her glove. And since now it's time to make an appearance at his friend's cocktail party a few blocks away, he pays, throws on his coat, and leaves.

As previously announced our man will remain nameless. It's easier to see himself from halfway across the room, literally and figuratively, an exercise he's given himself these past few weeks, looking hard and long at his reflection in, say, a storefront window and practicing seeing himself as a stranger, just some other man on the street. Because he notices he most often looks at his reflection and does not see himself as he is now but as the skinny and preoccupied young man he was at twenty-eight or thirty. So he suspects he'll learn something, maybe even grow as a human being if he can bear such a thing. Maybe he'll find the means to articulate that jumble of cheap but appealing insight he always has banging around inside his head just out of reach of a real desire to shape it, an uncertain stack of empty tin cans threatening to collapse about his feet, light, disposable, pointless maybe, but his all the same. Walking up Church Street with a biting wind at his back he realizes that, in fact, it's his simplicity, his suspected lack of depth, that compels him to look closer at this man. For the first time in his life, he thinks he has found a subject both suitably recognizable, himself, and deeply puzzling, also himself.

The party at his friend's loft is a fairly even mix of people fifty and older and those thirty and younger. His friend, Gunther, is a painter and most of the older set are associated with the arts as well: sculptors, writers, or museum and gallery curators. The younger guests are mostly students of the established professionals and who are now starting their own careers. Our man knows little but the superficialities of the art world and so listens attentively to conversation before venturing to ask anything that might allow him into the discussion gracefully. And this works well. Before long he's perfectly comfortable talking with anyone about many things he knows nothing about.

The first thing he notices on entering, however, is that this loft is now home to a woman as well as his friend the painter. He's been here a number of times over the years and has enjoyed the unmistakable male workshop vibe of it. But Gunther's girlfriend, Brooke, an accomplished choreographer, moved in a few months ago and the change is obvious. It's a place to live in now, practically civilized. It's pleasant but he'll miss the dignified funk the place had in the old days. Though Gunther lived and painted in it for over thirty years, there were few concessions to domesticity, just a table to eat at if one pushed aside the stacks of books and catalogues. Now there's matching stemware and cloth napkins, plenty of table space and chairs not splattered or streaked with paint.

Our man supposes it's sensible to make some adjustments. Men get weird if they live alone for too long. Apart from his own tendency to talk to himself, he recently found he was about to go out the door, his coat already on, before a chance glance in the hallway mirror revealed he still had shaving cream down one side of his face. Apparently, he'd had some great idea while performing his morning rituals and set down the razor immediately to write it out. Then he made coffee. Then he got dressed. Then he made to leave the house with shaving cream down one side of his face.

But now, here at this pleasant party in Tribeca, he's having a great conversation with a man named Aldo who writes about music. Aldo is in the early stages of writing a book about seven of the most influential but unsuccessful musicians of the twentieth century.

"Of course, the popular trends of music are fascinating and important to understand," Aldo explains. "But a lot of that is underpinned by music that never got to the surface, so to speak. In that sense, and not as an adopted style, it really is underground. There are some very influential musicians who were not successful in a popular sense but whose achievements propelled a lot of what we listen to more widely."

And now they're interrupted by Aldo's wife, Lisa, and their friend, a gallery owner named Tom, both of whom have just realized our hero is the filmmaker whose work they think so highly of. As you can imagine it's a nice moment for our man but he'd really prefer to hear Aldo continue about popularly unsuccessful over-achievers. And then Brooke is there before them with more wine, pouring, drinking, the subject somehow redirected to the recent presidential election and everyone's relieved the president is still in office.

"Maybe he'll be able to get something done now."

"Hardly a liberal victory."

"I mean, really, he's essentially an Eisenhower republican."

"And that," someone concurs with a sigh, "is about as left as an elected American official can get these days."

During all this our man is captivated by a woman whose

name he learns is Anne. She's lingering at the edge of the conversation, smiling timidly. She's a contemporary of Gunther's which puts her probably in her early sixties. She has a pretty and very girlish face, a wide inviting mouth done up tastefully in an aggressive red lipstick, sparkling dark eyes and a slim figure. Her abundant hair is a delightful storm of white and dark grays arranged with care but appearing haphazard. She knows she's good-looking and is used to this perhaps inconvenient adjunct to her artistic career. He imagines it's often a bore, though she has condescended to be stunning this evening. And, if he's not mistaken, she is appreciating him being caught up in the cloud of her attractions.

Is he hitting on this woman?

Is that allowed?

Is she reciprocating?

He's a little dizzy from this perilous little foray into mature situations by the time he notices it's seven o'clock. Some of the younger people are leaving to move on to other parties. He thinks he should leave too before he does something irresponsible with Anne, to indicate more than he intends. It takes a good twenty minutes to get out of the loft because he has made three or four new friends of these artists and writers and there is a lot of searching for business cards and scribbling of email addresses.

~

Finally, he's on the subway riding back uptown before it occurs to him to ask: What are my intentions? Does he really want to woo this attractive painter and educator or does he just want more mature friends? He and Anne had not talked that much and when she did, for instance, describe her painting, he felt challenged. It was something about mathematics, equations or algorithms her students generate with computer programs that she then translates into color-field patterns. He nodded, interested but non-committal. Her manner, like his, though sincere, suggested they were just throwing language around while they checked each other out. Which may have been the case. Perhaps she did find him attractive. But her amusement was tinged with a kind of proud vulnerability that made him feel adolescent.

The number one Broadway local rattles and bangs its way north and, though he removes his book from his coat pocket, he decides not to return to his reading. He's content to sit back and watch the show. He loves riding the subway for the narrative potential of glimpsed situations. It's endless.

For example:

A young couple across from him on their way to a party, sitting side by side, thinking their own thoughts, together but alone. There's been a tiff, clearly. The young man would rather not go to this party at all but the girl has promised her friend. She stares at her knees, biting her lip, as her boyfriend hazards a glance to gauge her mood. He's not encouraged. He regrets—

What? our hero wonders. What could it be the young man regrets? What has he said? What self-centered and insensitive male *faux pas* perfectly pardonable in other, slightly different circumstances, has he let fly to wound their potentially pleasant evening? She's a mystery to him anyway but her place in his young life calms him, reassures him, gives him confidence, at least when she's not openly questioning his loosely held and casually proclaimed assumptions.

This kind of thing keeps our man entertained all the way up to 23rd Street where the couple exits. The young man has to reach for his girl's hand twice before she'll allow him to take it. Interesting.

That leaves him alone in the train to study the ads running the length of the car up near the ceiling. They're selling a local news program:

Are you tired of the same old evening news?

What's that supposed to mean, he wonders. Are they suggesting they'll find other, more exciting, local news besides what's actually happening?

Then, further to the right, another variation:

If you're thinking it, they're saying it.

Ah, so they'll tell him whatever they think he wants to hear.

There are four or five versions, all with expensively produced studio-lit photos of this cool, carefully designed, casually attractive group of news professionals. Their expressions are a triumph of open-minded engagement with the issues. But they're not righteous. No, they're smart and likeable, carefully arranged as to the color of their skin and healthily self-effacing. The whole thing seems to be congratulating our friend on both his intelligence and his frustration with the status quo which is conveniently and implicitly condemned, gently. No names are named. Everyone is free to decide for themselves what the impaired status quo is and who is responsible. Equal opportunity grievance. And inclusive. One is encouraged to believe these studied and well-groomed media professsionals will provide as much impassioned analysis of a dispute concerning inner city traffic laws as they will to the remorse of a local veteran of the latest American invasion who recently shot up a crowd of people in a restaurant. Because you know what? that's what democracy is all about. Thank you for your support. You deserve it. Etcetera.

He feels, again, oppressed by the ubiquity of calculated but noncommittal fault-free insinuation, the noise pollution of commodified engagement. And he's grateful when another young couple, long-limbed Hispanic teenagers, tumble in at 28th Street. They toss themselves into a corner seat at the end of the car and giggle like conspireators while they pet one another and share the earbuds of the cell phone the boy grips in his hand. Our man would like to assemble their story too for the simple pleasure of the exercise. But there's not enough time. He's expected at a reception in the lobby of the Museum of Modern Art in fifteen minutes where an acquaintance of his, a younger filmmaker, has premiered his most recent production. Our man's already seen the film but needs to make an appearance as it was he who suggested it to the programmer at the museum. It will be commercially released next Friday and this event is useful promotion. The Mistress is supposed to meet him there if she can arrange a babysitter. Then, after he has fulfilled his duty, they'll duck out and take a taxi up the Westside Highway to his place where they'll make love for an hour before he calls a car service to take her back home to her sleeping children on the Upper East Side.

He thinks he can manage this. And he must. These days it's getting more and more difficult to rendezvous. His

Mistress's husband is not the problem, a man totally uninterested in his gorgeous wife except wherein she functions as a needed appendage to his business dealings.

"I'm a trophy wife," she told him on their first real date, huddled like criminals behind a table at the back of a dim restaurant in the middle of the afternoon.

No, the difficulty spending time together increases in direct proportion to the height of her two little girls, twins arranged by a doctor for this attractive power couple. They require her presence, her collaboration and her advice a little bit more with every fraction of an inch they grow.

Arriving at the museum, he checks his coat, is handed a glass of champagne, and is immediately photographed with an elderly gentleman he's never seen before but who seems to be associated with the film. Nodding and smiling graciously, he moves on and spots Tom, the filmmaker. Tom is dryly holding forth on the casualness of his aesthetic to a journalist who is busy feeding on high-end finger food while a small crowd of the interested attend to Tom's every word.

"It just, you know, happens," the young man explains. "I write the script, talk to some people, and somehow the film just gets made." Then, frowning quizzically, he adds, "It's amazing, really. Kind of troubling."

No one knows how to take any of this. Is he joking? Is he lying? Is he dead serious? Our man has been terrified of this guy for years, never knowing how to engage in even the simplest exchange. But Tom clearly wanted to know him and initiated a correspondence, forthrightly asking for advice and critical input. And he was happy to try because he found Tom's films to be unusual and refreshing. The first one was funny and insightful. The second one just as funny, less insightful, but more confidently achieved. This, his third, is the best so far. Still, in conversation our man always feels he is missing a joke, is perhaps being made fun of, that he is seeing something unique and hard to name in the younger man's films that the younger man himself thinks is stupidly obvious.

Somehow, they've become friends.

"Ah, here is our man himself," Tom announces, and introduces him to the journalist. "I'm sure you know one another."

The journalist turns to our man and coughs. A drop of sour cream falls from his lip and splashes onto the face of the mobile device he's using as a recorder. Our hero once threw him into a pool at the Cannes Film Festival along with his camera. They do not shake hands.

"Hey," he says, "sorry about the you know."

"No prob," replies the journalist. "I'm over it." And he

wanders off into the crowd in search of more *hors d'oeuvres*. Tom might be seeing more in this than is merely apparent, for he's narrating events in real time:

"And he walks away, never to be heard from again."

"Sorry, Tom, that might manifest itself as bad ink."

"As long as it's properly punctuated and spell-checked, bad ink, too, has its uses. Are you alone?"

"I'm meeting the Mistress."

"Do you really call her the Mistress?"

"That's the way she wants it, *the* Mistress. She hasn't read a book from cover to cover in her life but she's very novelistic in a 19th century European kind of way."

"What does she call you?"

"I'm the Lover."

"That's just scandalous, I mean aesthetically and socio-politically." Then, reaching for another glass of champagne, gesturing to the young throng around them: "This is, as I'm sure you've guessed, my devoted East Coast fan base."

Our friend and elder statesman says hello, asks names, and listens to brief blushing recitals of résumés as Tom does his blasé dumb luck genius routine for a few late-arriving journalists. The young people our man meets are aspiring motion picture professionals, primarily actors and actresses. They have no idea who he is or why Tom values his good regard but they're very polite and well-adjusted people. Our man senses a singular lack of charisma in this gathering. But he's heard lack of charisma is the new charisma. So what's he know.

And then the Mistress arrives, causing her expected sensation. Heads turn in a wave preceding her, conversation stops, eyebrows are raised. She's used to all this, having been a fashion model since the age of thirteen. She moves from the coat check desk and through the lobby with a down-to-earth manner of walking on air that somehow conveys both appreciation for being admired and an assurance that no one will get hurt. The aspiring young professionals are impressed enough to ask one another who our hero is anyway to have a date like this. She's perfectly gracious and knows how to attend to conversation so that those involved strive for greater eloquence. And this helps a good deal as our man is now expected to answer a few questions from members of the press. The Mistress's imposing loveliness usefully skews various planes of significance.

One journalist makes sure Tom is listening as he asks our man aloud:

"So, do you think Tom is the next new thing?"

Our man glances at Tom and decides his answer should be just as flippant as the question.

"Of course, look at that haircut."

Everyone cracks up. This is, apparently, all that's required and he might be able to slip away with the Mistress without having to say anything meaningful. But another more earnest and important journalist presses closer and wants to know "really" what he thinks of the film. He knows she has already written a grudgingly mixed review of Tom's latest which will appear on Thursday in which she bemoans the continued use of irony by Tom, our man, and others like them, convinced as she is that it is, to use her words, solipsistic, elitist, and a willful disregard for the expectations and attitudes of mainstream audiences.

"Well, it certainly isn't manufactured product for a known market," our man replies, nodding, his words, like static electricity, sparking out in little snaps and crackles amongst those gathered.

It gets quieter. What more needs to be said?

Tom's new haircut can be seen to bristle but he smiles gamely. The Mistress twists two fingers into the back pocket of our man's trousers and tugs once, a sign she thinks he's getting in over his head. And of course he is in over his head. He always has been. He is in over his head and though he knows what he's talking about from one moment to the next he is never confident about how it addresses the bigger picture, if there is a bigger picture.

Some Olympian view of the vast landscape of commercial entertainment and the roiling societal indicators confidently articulated on social media is not necessarily something a creative person has at hand when, as often happens, he or she decides to stay still and remain gazing into the mess of human motive.

Not wishing to insult Tom obviously right there in public, the journalist craftily reformulates her criticism as an honest and well-intentioned question, not of Tom, however, but of his supportive contemporary.

"What do you think of people who say that a confident outsider stance is not much more than an abdication of professional will and an easy dilettantish posturing playing to the cheap seats of an already committed following?"

Wow! he thinks, she's good, a regular samurai. He glances over at Tom whose eyes go wide with excitement. Tom would love to see blood spilled here on the floor of the museum. The Mistress tugs again, finishes her champagne in one go, and smiles at a photographer.

Flash!

Faced with such incisive critical acumen in a public sort of way, our man finds himself tumbling mentally into something like an emotional whirlpool wherein he knows by experience he has his best ideas. The spirit seizes him and he looks on at himself speaking, as if he were at the top of the staircase to his left, and decides to leave the question unanswered and speak about something else entirely.

"I'm impressed by the determined and unflinching presentation of a world where everyone is so radically disconnected. It's funny but disturbing, merciless even. Relentlessly looking at common human foibles but never condescending. People say things to one another in this movie of Tom's that are brutal. But the manner in which these brutalities are phrased, how they're framed, something about the lightness of how they're presented, is humane. Affectionately bleak. Not unheard of in, say, for instance, Balzac."

He glances at Tom for permission.

"Go for it, dude."

The area has fallen silent now, champagne everywhere held aloft mid-sip, finger food abandoned, the Mistress still tugging.

"In this film, making the attempt to connect is at best an accident and always misguided. Tom's achievement here, I think, is the unapologetic suggestion that human isolation is the primary subject worth considering seriously, particularly if we want to console one another."

~

The next thing he knows he's in a taxi speeding north along the Hudson with the Mistress's tongue in his mouth and his hand thrust in beneath her pantyhose. The driver is talking to his relatives back in Pakistan and doesn't notice these two schedule-challenged consenting adults making love there on the back seat of his means of employment. They can talk and compare notes on their past week's petty dramas when they arrive at his place.

Outside his address, she stumbles from the cab, straightening her skirt, while he pays the driver. As he himself stands up out of the cab she zips up his fly for him before turning to see his neighbors standing on the sidewalk, a nice, friendly older couple out walking their matching dachshunds.

"Hi," he says.

"Hi," the Mistress adds sheepishly, dragging a few strands of her long black hair from off her smudged lipstick.

"Hi," the couple reply hesitantly and move off.

TWO

Waking early on Sunday morning, he travels back downtown on the subway to Pennsylvania Station. From there, he'll transfer to the Long Island Rail Road and take a train out to his hometown. He spends three days a week now with his eighty-seven-year-old dad, cooking in the evening and doing whatever lifting and carting might be needed around the house throughout the day. The past few years have been touch-and-go for the old man. He seemed about to expire two summers ago but bounced back, though he's still often alarmingly frail.

Our man has always felt oddly comforted in Penn Station, this huge and soulless train wreck of city planning. For him it's one of the few constants in the various phases of his life and career, a transfer depot he's always obliged to reenter no matter how poor or rich he is at the time.

And on these weekly trips out to look after his dad he always schedules an hour to hang out in a little bookstore across from Track 21, Penn Books. For the most part its main purpose is to cash in on bestsellers targeted to busy commuters thirsty for distraction. But many years ago he discovered that there is a literature section way in back against a wall normally stacked with cardboard boxes awaiting removal. This literature section is not at all bad. For instance, all he owns of Samuel Beckett, Henry Miller, Graham Greene, Edith Wharton, and George Elliot was purchased here. He appreciates the need to elbow one's way past ghost-written celebrity bios and manufactured romances to find, wow! a marked-down remaindered paperback of Simone Weil's *Gravity and Grace*! Yes, if with patience and cunning one pokes around long enough, one discovers a philosophy shelf down low to the floor beneath the self-help and exercise books.

So now he investigates casually and wanders over to a section headed *Career Opportunities*. He wants to know what people think about when they choose, or are forced, to find a new job. Because he suspects he's outlived his viability in the filmmaking racket and wouldn't mind finding a new vocation for himself. There are various bright, happy, point-by-point manuals encouraging any regular Joe with the requisite focus and determination to become an entrepreneur. Find something you like and know how to do and go for it! That seems to be the big message. A few books are a bit more specific and technical about, for instance, setting up online businesses, applying for merchant accounts with banks so as to process credit cards and so on, how to promote one's brand.

He wants to try something new, something different. He's become a good manager, at least of a small arts-related business such as his own, and wishes he could hit upon an idea for a small useful product capable of being sold to millions of people, enough to sustain a small factory somewhere.

"Guns," said his good friend, Jesus, the superintendent of his building.

"You think I should manufacture guns?"

"Just saying," Jesus shrugged. "More like import-export. Around here that's how it used to be: guns, drugs, and girls. All the guys with the serious money were involved in one or the other." Then, pausing for emphasis, Jesus added: "Or all three, because they're related."

Jesus doesn't, for some reason, pronounce his name in the Spanish manner: *hey-zeus*. He walks up, offers his big boney worker's hand and says, "Hi, I'm Jesus." Always disconcerting no matter how many times our man hears it.

Jesus lives in the basement of the building with his wife, Lucille, his mother and his aunt, both old ladies from the Dominican Republic. Lucille is a local New York girl, Puerto Rican, a class-A harridan. The neighbors suspect she is the ringleader of a small gang of teenage thieves.

"I was thinking more along the lines of some custom-designed USB thumb drives."

"Well, you be the man," Jesus conceded, raising his hands, palms out, leading the way through the basement to his tool room where they knocked around through a pile of old light switches, door knobs, and faucet handles, looking for a hinge that would fit the standard medicine cabinet most of the apartments came with. "Why do you want to be a factory owner," he asked, searching, "You being like this famous film director an' shit."

Our man took in the immensity of the clutter in the tiny, dark, windowless room. "I was famous for about eighteen months twenty years ago," he admitted, coughing, waving away dust. "Now, you know, I'm just sort of respected." He clicked on a hanging work lamp and backed away from the glare, making a visor of his arm. "Here, look," he said, discovering a pile of hinges. The two of them started sorting through these, comparing their sizes and shapes with the busted one he'd brought down from the apartment.

"The lady in C45 says you're a national treasure," Jesus insisted clumsily.

"What?"

"She said so. Just that way. 'National treasure.'"

Our man shook his head and pushed his hands into the pile of rusting parts, spreading them more thinly over the oil-stained wooden work bench. "I got a medal once from the French," he admitted. "But I think it was a mistake."

"That's it," Jesus exclaimed, victorious, grabbing a hinge and holding it up. Our man compared it to the busted one he had in his hand and nodded.

"Great. Thanks, pal."

"Da nada, maestro."

As the train rolls along through the early morning Sunday of Queens he looks out at the factory buildings and other assorted industrial structures he's looked out at from this train all his life. To him it has always been just so much urban blight and featureless utilitarian commercial desert. He never sees human beings down there, just train yards, dark warehouses, gravel pits, an occasional fenced-in parking lot filled with garbage trucks. Industry, he thinks. Find something you can make well and sell responsibly to people who need it. How hard can that be?

Pulling into town about an hour later he exits the train

and comes down from the elevated platform to the street. Crossing to the far sidewalk he stops and looks to his right when a car lightly honks at him. It's his childhood friend, Kurt, who works for the local power company. Kurt pulls the company car over to the curb.

"Hey!"

"Hey, man. What, they got you working on Sunday?"

"Every day of the week since this fucking hurricane bullshit. What do we pay taxes for anyway!? This is New York. We're not even supposed to *have* hurricanes! How's your dad, okay?"

"Yeah, he's fine. Power down for a day or two but all he uses electricity for is to watch the Yankees and their game was cancelled so, you know, it was all just weather to him."

"You need a ride?"

"No, thanks. I'll walk."

"You sure," Kurt asks, concerned, casting a glance around the area like maybe they're about to complete a drug deal. "People talk, you know."

"About what?"

"They wonder why you walk from the station to your dad's house. Trish what's her name the wife of that asshole. I checked their meter Tuesday. She says she saw you walking back from the supermarket with an armful of groceries and everything."

"I like to walk. It's only five blocks away."

Kurt gets out of the car and lights a cigarette. "Hey, sure, look, I've known you since little league. But other people, you know, they think maybe you've had your license revoked." Not to drive around here is to be half a person. Our man understands his friend's concern. "These over-medicated stay-at-home broads," Kurt adds, "are certain you're a degenerate or something, maybe did time for some sick show biz related perversion too weird even for the tabloids."

Our man's a little flattered, imagining various high school heartthrobs of note, now in their middle years, paging through magazines at the checkout counter looking to see if he's fathered some glossy celebrity's love child. "Look, don't set them straight on that, okay." Then, continuing on his way, he calls back, "Let them stay up at night worrying!"

"Ha!" Kurt laughs as he gets back in behind the wheel. "Nothing at all worries these bored and horny dames but wrinkles!"

Kurt would know, our man supposes. He was always great with the girls. He got laid first, before any of their friends, scoring with one of their substitute teachers in junior high school. It's impossible for him to imagine Kurt enduring a moment of helpless sentiment or selfless wonder at a woman's beauty, grace, or even her sexual power. His pleasure is somehow in his uncaring. He's got a wife whom he can't stand and three grown kids, one in college. But he's still good-looking and obviously on the prowl, though with what often smells like a grievance.

And despite his waffling commitment to exit show biz and find a new vocation for himself, our man, as he walks the five blocks home, falls to the one plow he knows best and begins to compose in his head ideas for a movie about a power company meter reader erotically tangled up with all the married women in town, the inevitable hilarious drama that ensues: mid-afternoon sex, fistfights, drunken car chases, heartrending confessions in the parking lots of strip malls.

To hell with this industrial manufacturing nonsense!

But by the time he gets to the house it's a different story altogether. His dad is standing in the middle of the kitchen gazing abstractedly at the linoleum floor. Hoping this is not some sort of neurological wipeout, our hero pauses before venturing quietly: "Dad?"

The old man looks up, blinks, then continues buttoning the cuff of his shirt sleeve. He seems to be getting ready to go somewhere.

“Jim’s in the hospital.”

“What?”

“Collapsed at work.”

Jim’s our man’s older brother, sixty-two.

He’s on the couch all of a sudden, having had something like a calm breathless blackout himself, not remembering how he got there. His father wavers in the doorway watching him, maybe wondering if he, too, his younger son, is about to buckle and break.

A moment later, the old man’s only daughter pulls up in her SUV with her teenage son and they all head off to the hospital. She’s just turned fifty and is a healthcare professional who, apart from her day job, pretty much runs the doctor-and-insurance-related obstacle course which is their father’s life these days. It’s good to have her around now that the war has opened up on a second front.

“Working even on Sunday,” our man asks, trying to piece together the narrative so far.

“Every day since the hurricane,” his sister replies, speeding east along Montauk Highway, a busy strip of asphalt four lanes wide he knows every inch of since the age of five. “They have to get the ATMs out of all the flooded areas.”

Their older brother works for a nationwide bank and for about twenty years has been in charge of the care and maintenance of their off-premises ATM machines. The recent hurricane has demolished many communities along the coast and ATMs loaded with cash are lying on their sides beneath a few feet of water in partially destroyed retail properties throughout Long Island. Now they have to retrieve these machines and return the paper money to the Federal Reserve. It's been twelve days since the storm and they've been working around the clock.

At the hospital, they're allowed into the emergency room one at a time to see Jim. But they allow the old man to go in escorted by his grandson. Our man sits beside his sister and marvels at the functioning of this huge bureaucracy which somehow the most maimed, feeble, addled, and outright stoned seem to be able to negotiate without too much trouble. In fact, they seem right at home. His sister certainly does. She takes up a seat and positively relaxes. This is her domain, an environment she feels comfortable in.

Since he's of no use to anyone in a situation like this, he uses the time to study the world around him. Hospitals, he admits, are foreign to him. He's rarely had health insurance, always baffled by the paperwork, the complexity of the procedures for making a claim, the sheer defensive aggression of the administrators, the cost.

"If I haven't mentioned it in passing, thanks for managing everything with dad these past few months."

"Oh, thanks," his sister smiles and shrugs, pleased but rueful. "It's what I do all day at work anyway."

"It's complicated and time consuming."

"I don't know how people do it without being trained professionals," she says out the side of her mouth, shaking her head. She's like a soldier of the healthcare bureaucracy, there to help save lives but knowing only the smart, lucky and tough will survive.

His niece, Eleanor, Jim's daughter, arrives just as Jim's wife comes out from the emergency room. They too both work in the healthcare field in various capacities. He's fascinated to listen to the women of the family discuss the hurricane and the practical fallout that's ensued. Someone sits down immediately to his left and he discovers Kurt, thin, wiry, taut, clutching his pack of cigarettes and a disposable lighter. He's watching our man listen to his relatives.

"Hey."

"How'd you hear?"

"Didn't. Just figured it out coming in. The wife's inside with some kind of heart disease medication upgrade or some shit. What's it, the old man?"

"No, it's Jim."

“What the fuck.”

“Collapsed at work.”

“Shit. Who’s that beside your sister?”

“My niece, Eleanor.”

“Fine looking piece of…”

“Hey, you can’t smoke in here.”

Kurt looks at the cigarette he’s instinctively raised to his lip while admiring Eleanor’s figure, the lighter poised for ignition. “Oh shit, sorry.” Lowering his preferred medication to his lap, he chucks his jaw towards the ladies. “They know what they’re talking about, though.”

“Yeah, they’re all in it too, the healthcare biz.”

“God bless them but good fucking luck. The state just admitted the biggest problem they got right now is theft and fraud. I could’ve told you that. The American way. Plunder, it’s anyone’s right provided they get away with it. People stealing Red Cross supplied materials, independent electrical contractors advertising themselves as federally licensed and approved, charging extortionist prices for immediate repairs people believe they’ll be reimbursed for, hospitals and county offices set up to provide material and financial assistance but can’t give anything useful away because people want what they cannot be given, toys for their children, cases of Coca-Cola, hood ornaments for their goddamn cars.”

Our hero, our representative regular guy, suspects his old friend might be an honest-to-god crank. But he's more than certain the man is just rattled about his wife. He feels he'll be able to make himself useful by simply lending an ear to his friend's burgeoning outrage.

"You want to step outside and smoke? I can use some air too."

"Who's in charge? Who do I sue? That's as far as fellow-feeling goes in this here republic. The social contract: screw or be screwed."

By now they're out at the edge of the parking lot watching people come and go. Our man has accepted a cigarette to be sociable but just let's it burn down unattended as Kurt lets off steam. Though his friend avoids expressing the remotest concern for his wife, he is clearly on edge, unsettled.

"Look at this mob. Everyone, White, Black, Asian, Hispanic, they're overweight and pasty-faced, the most unhealthy-looking population I've ever seen in person or on TV. And these are not the patients but their families and loved ones, the un-sick just coming to visit." He lights his second cigarette and considers the parked automobiles stretched out to the horizon. "Driving here you see the same thing, people walking from their cars to the stores, large, ungainly, impaired by excess, I think the saying goes. You don't see anyone—except you, of course—walking anywhere, though there are sidewalks, relics, perhaps, of some forgotten civilization, the great outdoors being the distance between one's car and the store one buys more unhealthy shit in. Thc houses too, the offices, the commercial buildings, the cheapest construction, made with the flimsiest materials, renovated in the most inefficient manner and in the worst possible taste."

Kurt, though with only a by-the-seat-of-his-pants high school education, is still widely read and, though often crude, well-spoken. And what he hasn't learned from books he's intuited. He was the one of the two most people thought would go to college and become something to write home about, an engineer or a pilot, maybe even a businessman or politician. He was naturally smart with a fast analytical mind and dependable instincts. The hero of our story on the other hand was kindly referred to as talented, sensitive, thoughtful, a person destined maybe for the priesthood, academia, or the arts. As a teenager, our friend relied strongly on Kurt's ability to think whereas Kurt always depended on his pal's tendency to understand. They each had closer friends, kids they spent more time with but none who were as curious about the wider world. Work prospects, wife prospects, new car prospects; these represented the outer limits of their circle's world view.

"You know. You've been everywhere," Kurt continues, stepping backwards off the curb and taking in the cheap disposable facade of the hospital. "I bet the poorest villages in Europe, Asia, or even Latin America have more dignity, ingenuity and community spirit than this cut-rate American middleclass suburban bullshit."

"What's your wife's name?"

"Kitty."

"Anyone I know from back in the day?"

"No, I met her after you left town. She was a teller in a bank in Babylon. Made extra money dancing topless at this place out here on the highway that's now a car dealership. Pain in the ass. Big as a house. Born again. Horrible."

"Your turn!"

Our man looks over and sees his niece offering him the little plastic badge one needs to enter the emergency room and see the patient.

"Kurt, I'll see you around. All the best for Kitty."

"Say hi to Jim for me."

Back inside he discovers another niece has arrived as well as a cousin and his wife. But his sister is missing.

"She's gone to get some coffees at the Starbucks near maternity," Eleanor explains.

Yes, it dawns on him now, the hospital feels exactly like a shopping mall. And it's like the beginnings of a party there in the waiting room, everyone so comfortable and familiar. His family has merged with two others nearby and there is much passing back and forth of mobile devices as they coo and smile at pictures of slobbering infants and toddlers with toy guns.

Though Eleanor has given him precise directions about where to find her father, our man enters the emergency room overwhelmed and promptly gets lost. He moves uncertainly through the congested space, around the wheeled diagnostic machinery, moveable curtain partitions and many exhausted unplugged people. He doesn't know which of these temporary cubicles his brother is in and he has to glance in at many. The whole thing is heartbreaking: a tiny old lady with a tube up her nose lying on her side and staring up at the ceiling in calm bewilderment; a young woman with a bloated, reddened face and a black eye; a skinny effeminate middle-aged man, pale and shivering, whimpering alone; a six-year-old girl clawing desperately to get out of her mother's arms as a nurse tries to affix a plastic mask over her mouth and nose. He feels perfectly guilty for intruding on these private miseries.

When he finds Jim, he practically runs to his older brother for absolution. But Jim is drifting in an out of consciousness, dazed, it seems, by a fierce headache.

"Hey."

"Who is that?" Jim barks, squinting.

Our man is terrified, certain his brother is doomed.

"It's me," he says, waving his hand before Jim's eyes to determine if he's aware of anything at all. "Can you see that? Can you see my hand?"

"I can't see anything with that damn light over there shining right in my eyes!"

Our man looks where indicated and sees a very wide circular lamp suspended from a large steel armature. It's got a heavy base with wheels and seems to have been shoved aside and rolled out of the way during the tussle with the little girl. It is, in fact, shining right down into Jim's face. He steps over, reaches out, finds the switch, sure he's going to be reprimanded, and turns it off.

Nothing happens. No one screams at him.

"Thank you. Wow, that's better."

Jim no longer seems at death's door. But he does look tired and he speaks with effort, like his mouth is numb.

"What happened," our man asks simply.

"I don't know. I felt crappy when I woke up. But I went to work and then, after half an hour or so, I went to get a coffee and felt like a drunk, bouncing off the walls, slurring my words. I couldn't even lift the coffee cup off the counter. I sat down and then, I don't know, they took me here."

He spends about ten minutes with Jim, not sure if it's okay to tire him out by having him retell his little adventure or if maybe it is, in fact, a good idea to keep his mind focused in just this way.

"You staying out at Dad's," Jim asks.

"Yeah."

"If you get a chance, can you set up those wireless phones we got him for Christmas last year?"

"Of course."

"He keeps saying he'll do it himself and he don't. But it's getting dangerous for him to walk through the kitchen and all the way down the hallway to answer the phone on the wall by the bathroom whenever we gotta talk to him."

"They're coming this week to install the life-alert gadget too."

"Right, and that attaches somehow to the phone. So we gotta get..." And he winces, looking away, trying to clench his jaw but his mouth is not cooperating. Our man steps closer, reaching out but not knowing what to touch or how to help.

"What is it?"

"Just these, this..." and Jim waits while something moves through his skull like a freight train made of razor-blades. When it passes, he looks up and shakes his head clear. "Every once in a while. I don't know."

"Maybe you were poisoned."

Now Jim looks at our man, his younger brother the filmmaker, and laughs silently, just shaking like a small underweight Santa Claus. When did his hair go all white?

"What, d'ya think this is a spy movie or something!"

"No, but they were saying how you guys have to get all the money out of the machines and clean it."

Jim suddenly gets all serious, this is something he finds fascinating and wants to describe.

"It's wild! We have to clean the money or the Feds won't take it. So we rent these huge laundry machines and chuck the bills in there. But then they gotta be dried flat and slow or the bills shrink, so..."

"But that's what I'm talking about, all that money has been lying around in water that's probably, from what I hear on the news, sixty or seventy percent sewage."

"It ain't pretty," Jim concurs, "that's for sure."

"Anyone else you work with get sick?"

"Chuck, but Chuck's always sick."

"Okay. Look, I'll be around. There's a crowd outside wanting to see you. The hospital says they'll be able to get you a room in a few hours."

"Yeah, okay," Jim nods. "Send in Eleanor. I need some comic relief."

"You don't find me entertaining?"

"You're too intellectual and not mainstream enough. They said so in the paper."

"I just made you laugh and look like an elf high on crack."

"That's true. But Eleanor's better looking."

He thinks it's amazing his brother has the presence of mind to reach directly for the best and simplest things in life at moments of maximum anxiety. He doesn't remember him like that in their youth. Back then it was maximum anxiety all the time, standing silently, poised to flee, ears cocked for signs of the next approaching disaster. Where did he get this laidback confidence from? Resigned, hopeful, not a shred of indignation. As our man turns away, Jim calls him back so he can demonstrate the cool device clamped on his finger that registers all his vital signs on the nearby monitor and which actually permits the "smart-bed" to operate in all its complexity.

"You take this little clamp thing off your finger and in two minutes an electrician, a cop, and nurse show up at the foot of the bed. Incredible."

~

Driving back from the hospital, his head still crowded with the sharp edges and blunt surfaces of Kurt's harangue, our man stops off with the family at the Sea Haven. The most well-intentioned of affordable restaurants, the Sea Haven caters to the sixty-five and over crowd that makes up so much of the local population these days. Pensioned retirees flock to the place between five and seven to eat more of the heavy, enriched and artificially preserved food that has probably sent each of them to the hospital countless times. Our man is shocked once again at how large people are out here. He marvels at how they have accommodated the discomfort of being overweight and how they get on with their lives as if being that uncomfortable were normal. Of course, they attenuate the discomfort with prescribed medications and the restaurant, like all local eateries, has been fitted out with larger seats to accommodate the added bulk.

His dad is, in fact, a slim guy. But he takes eleven different medications every day. He had a heart attack in his late sixties and walked away after surgery with the ticker of a man half his age. He hasn't had a drink in over forty years. And if he'd just walk up the street to the corner twice a day to exercise his—

But our friend has to shut off this stream of complaint coursing through him and attempt to be civil. He studies the menu and tries to find the least enriched, least flavored, least fried food available. He decides on the fillet of sole which, in his experience, is a simple broiled piece of white fish one squeezes lemon on.

But not here. The Sea Haven's fillet of sole is covered with some sort of thick sauce and comes with a mound of french-fries and a boiled, completely tasteless, chunk of broccoli.

And, of course, the news.

The current mainstream news channel on three different overhead flat-screen televisions is staging a roundtable discussion amongst their on-air staff, scripted debate wherein the various well-groomed personalities express opinions culled from their demographic research as if simply musing. "Tossing it out there," one of them says, attractively open-minded and displaying only as much conviction as needed to illustrate that one is allowed to, and admired for, having an opinion. But, of course, they don't have opinions. They are entertainers playing their roles of engaged journalists. They even have, this evening, a debate about responsible journalism that is perfectly scripted to portray them as concerned and diligent and of course always only human, people who see the sense, it's implied, in more conservative outlooks. Then they cut to commercials for credit cards, fast food, automobiles and various medications.

He has three hesitant mouthfuls of the sole and pretends he has to use the men's room. In fact, he passes the bar, shakes hands with the owner's son, Alexi, who he went to high school with, and ducks into the parking lot out back. He just needs air, some psychic space not invaded by inanity. Of course, he knows as well as anyone he is popularly regarded as a hyper-sensitive and rarified elitist, maybe not even all that patriotic. He doesn't feel the need to apologize because he has, in fact, spent twenty-five years making work which frankly discloses his confused good intentions and pathetically inadequate moral outrage. He'd hate to come off like a know-it-all. But he's not ashamed to appear worried.

There are two overweight guys in the parking lot smoking beside their van. *Certified Pro Painters* is written across its side. They all nod hello to one another. The younger of the two offers our man a smoke.

"No thanks. Just getting some air."

"You're the guy, right?" the older painter says, "the guy who makes movies and shit?"

Grinning, he nods. "Yeah, that's me."

"They got your autographed picture in there near the bar."

"Yeah, that was years ago," he replies and, trying to

change the subject, asks, "Do you have to be certified professional to paint houses out here these days?"

The two men look at him and blink. They don't know what he's talking about. He gestures to their van.

"'Certified Pro.' I thought it must mean, you know, certified professional."

The two painters consider the words there on the side of their van as if for the first time.

"That's just the name of the company," says the older of the two at last. But the younger guy is still intrigued about our man's autographed picture in by the bar.

"What kind of movies you make?"

Now he's just eager to get back inside.

"Oh, you know, just..." and he gives up and says what is at once perfectly true but somehow totally beside the point, "romantic comedies."

He goes back inside but doesn't want to rejoin the family. He stops in the bar area and looks out at his sister, nephew, and dad, all talking animatedly about different commercials on the various televisions. He doesn't want to impose on their enthusiasm. They are so much more relaxed when he is not amongst them.

"Hey!"

Our man looks to his left and sees Kurt at the bar, still in his power company overalls. Our friend is delighted, grateful, and afraid all at once. But he joins him.

"You looking to get laid," Kurt asks.

"If only," our man admits, sadly. "My sister and dad are in there with my nephew."

"Yeah, well, this place don't start hoppin' till after eight when all the oldsters stumble off home."

Kurt is glowing with some kind of weird inner light.

"Are you high?"

"Stoned immaculate since mid-afternoon," his friend confesses proudly. "A mix of some of this nonsense the wife takes for her depression and the stuff my daughter takes for her bi-polar disorder." Handing our man a fresh cold frosty, and paying for it, he adds: "With a shot of vodka it's a fucking beautiful high."

Taking the beer, our man drinks, buying time to think.

"Thanks, man."

"You want some," Kurt asks, spilling some pills out from his chest pocket.

"No, I've got to be on call for the old man in case he decides to jump off the roof in the middle of the night."

Our man is comforted that this cracks up his very high old friend so thoroughly. He waits while Kurt gets his shit together again and drinks.

"It's true, though," Kurt finally insists, "these old bastards go all sex mad in their eighties."

"No!" our man protests, hoping against hope, but actually needing input. "You're kiddin' me."

"My old man, not even as old as yours, he gets this heart tremor, goes to the hospital and starts raving about all these diabolical orgies the nurses are perpetrating while he's trying to sleep!"

"Oh shit, I've heard about this." And he has.

"Same all over. You get these cranky old farts on ten to twenty different meds daily and once they're in a hospital, away from home, they start seeing crazy-assed sex all over the place!"

Alexi, behind the bar, is nodding his head, sadly, commiserating. The Greek gentleman places the flat of his hand against his heart to demonstrate mutual experience and understanding. Apparently, they're all in this together.

Our hero slides off his stool and looks through the glass partition that separates the bar from the dining room. He studies his old man. Kurt joins him.

"You think so," he asks.

"Dude, we're all just animals."

"Even him?" gesturing to his dad.

But our man's dad seems to pose a unique challenge to Kurt's otherwise blanket but admiring condemnation of the male species as little more than sex-mad scavengers. He frowns.

"He still go to church?"

"At least on Sundays."

"Oh that don't count." Kurt sits back at the bar and our man follows. "He's just a guy after all. A man like any other," then, quoting deliriously, "'If you prick me, do I not bleed?'"

"Yeah, Shakespeare had it all figured out."

"Who?"

But Kurt did in fact read *The Merchant of Venice* and not just to pass third year English. He dwelt on it, sometimes quoted it, and preferred it to *Henry V*. Our man couldn't get through five or six pages of either one of these plays and passed third year English only because he never missed a class and was too shy to start any kind of trouble.

"Remember when I made you tell me the whole story of *Henry V* so I wouldn't have to read the thing myself?"

"But you passed the test, right?"

"With a C-plus," our man remembers proudly, "the best grade I ever got in high school!"

"And the main character has your own goddamned name, for cryin' out loud!" Kurt shakes his head, then: "You were really a dense kid. These days they'd call you autistic or something and you'd be getting scholarships. I'm sure my number two son is brain-damaged and he's in his second year at Oberlin."

He's halfway through his second beer and Kurt is nursing a martini, buoyed blissfully by the mix of prescribed mood enhancers he's stolen from home.

"You come here often?"

"Few times a week," Kurt allows, scanning the retreating retirees, anticipating the influx of the after-eight crowd. "There's this real estate bitch I hook up with occasionally. A real slut. Wants it all dramatic and stuff, like with ropes and blindfolds and everything. I'm hoping she swings by tonight."

Our man leans back a little on his stool, blinks, and lowers his beer to the bar, misses, and tries again. This accomplished, he leans in closer, concerned.

"Things that bad at home, huh?"

"Actually, things are good at home. I bought this deluxe pre-made log cabin with a bathroom I set up in the backyard and moved into that about ten years ago. Don't talk to wife—ever. That dumb cunt. My daughter is the go-between. And as far as pussy goes, I fuck all these married bitches during the day when I read their meters."

It's been some time since our hero has heard such easily held, unselfconscious, and rude sexist invective. He's not entertained but he is interested, the professional entertainer in him speaking up before he knows what's happening.

"You should write a book."

"Dude, I could tell you stories that would make you a rich man."

"Though maybe not particularly loved."

"Damn straight, fuck love! Enough of this artsy philosophical bullshit you're famous for. Make a movie about the garbage I wade through every day and let's get rich."

Our man sees his family getting up from the table, stands, and tosses a twenty on the bar.

"Look, I gotta go. Let's talk about this some more."

Kurt doesn't seem to be aware he has suggested something our man takes seriously. He's got his eye trained on the front entrance where a stylishly dressed forty-year-old woman with a small badge above her breast pocket reading *Dial Real Estate* is checking her coat.

Getting back to the house our man sits down to watch professional football on TV. Though his mind is elsewhere and he thinks he's just keeping the old man company for confused reasons of his own, he finds himself deeply involved in the game. He has watched a lot of pro football these past few years with Dad and has relearned the rules. The game speaks to him in ways he doesn't dare explain to his extended family. It's personal. Twenty-five years of professional filmmaking has attuned him to the exquisite drama of executing beautiful strategy in the teeth of brutal opposition. He feels for the offense, for the quarterback, prays for the successful completion of the play at hand. He doesn't even have a favorite in this race. He sides with who's ever losing at that moment, on the edge of his seat, tense with expectation.

And this cracks Dad up. Or disquiets him. It's hard to tell.

The play is called. The ball is snapped. It's a faked hand-off before a short pass that's caught, nearly fumbled, retrieved and, at last, a gain of five yards. He thinks he and Dad might actually experience ninety or so seconds of real male bonding.

After the game, the old guy, probably thinking he owes his son some payback for enduring an evening of televised sport, channel-surfs and looks for a movie, stumbling into *Sullivan's Travels* from 1941. Our man sits up, alert.

"Oh hey stop that's good. You'll like it. *Sullivan's Travels* with Joel McCrae and Veronica Lake."

"Is it a comedy?"

"Yeah. It's hilarious."

But, in fact, the film is well along and deep into its infamous dark part, a twenty-minute section expatiating upon the true sadness and squalor of the depression. He finds himself subjecting his enfeebled dad to the grimmest scenes of avoidable hunger, homelessness, and despair imaginable in a mainstream Hollywood entertainment. But after that there's a few good jokes and he sees the old guy laugh when Veronica Lake pushes McCrae into a swimming pool. When it's over, the old man gets up and begins shuffling off to bed. He grins, satisfied, and asks:

"Who's the girl?"

"Veronica Lake."

"She's funny," the old man says as he bends back to drop a few splashes of prescription moisturizer into each eye. Recapping the small bottle and placing it back in the fridge, he makes his way down the hall to his room. "Good night," he calls faintly and our man thinks he sees something like a new spring in the old guy's step.

Is it possible a pretty girl in an old movie on TV is enough to make this aged guy forget his many aches and pains?

Maybe.

And thank goodness for it. Such an easy balm for the bumps and scrapes of inevitable decay.

He heads up to his boyhood room with a cold bottle of beer he finds at the back of the fridge. Twisting off the cap, he kicks his boots up onto the radiator. As he's about to drink, his cellphone rings. He gets up and finds it in the pocket of his jacket, assuming it's bad news like Jim has taken a turn for the worse or his father has somehow wandered out of the house downstairs and been found saying rude things to promiscuous nurses hanging around outside the delicatessen. Who knows?

"Hello," he asks wearily.

"Hi. You found my glove."

The voice is a lovely cascade of tones. Is someone singing to him? He's confused.

"Excuse me," he says, clearing his head.

"My glove. In the bistro. Your card was inside."

"Ah!" he stands back and straightens up. Smiling, he nods. "I see. Well, I'm glad it's not still lost."

"It's not. Thank you," she assures him in a voice he thinks is flirtatious. After all, he left his card inside the glove. That can only be interpreted as a come-on. There's a moment of silence, each of them assessing the other's pause. He's certain she doesn't want to get off the line. Then she says, "I was surprised to find out who you were."

Panicked, his first thought is: Who am I? What does she know? But he calms down and realizes: "Oh, yes, well..." He trails off, at sea, wishing he could go back to drinking his beer in the dark beside the radiator.

"My parents know your films well."

Indeed, her parents! She's young enough to be his own

daughter. He's got to get off the line. But she continues, sensitive, it seems, to how that last statement might have fallen wrongly:

"I don't follow films that much myself but my friend takes a cinema history course and they study one of your movies."

"Where do you study," he asks, desperate to change the subject.

"NYU," she announces plainly but with the hint of a lilt, a slight modulation of the "U," and he thinks he hears the product of an English public-school education.

"Where are you from?"

"Michigan, mostly."

"I heard your parents speaking French."

"Oh, that was my uncle. And my mom, yes. That side of the family, my mom's, is from Montreal. And, yes, of course, my mom teaches French at the university."

"In Michigan."

"Ann Arbor, yes."

During this, he wanders back to the radiator and retrieves his beer, enjoying himself.

"What are you studying?"

"Nothing in particular," she chimes. "Just my foundation courses. I'm a freshman who started late. But I'm enjoying my survey courses, particularly English Literature."

"You sound pretty literate."

"Do I," she asks laughing lightly. And he can tell, expensive or on the cheap, this girl has got an old-school education.

"You do," he confirms and takes a swig of his beer.

"Hm," she muses, then, "It's because my parents are educated. Both teachers, in fact."

"What's your dad teach?"

"Economics. We spend a lot of time in England because he lectures at the London School Of."

Bingo.

"And what about you," she asks and he can hear her resettling herself on—who knows—the banquette behind the table of a cafe, a couch, her bed?

"You mean what do I study," he teases her.

"No!" she laughs but then, adjusting, all serious: "Well, maybe. I guess people continue to study, right?

"My agent, Edward, calls me the eternal student."

"I think I read that."

"Excuse me?"

"I googled you," she admits.

Feeling exactly like one does when handed a ticket for someone else's traffic violation, our man sighs and drinks. But again, alert to shifts in temperament, she hurries to qualify:

"I would have called you sooner but I was finding all these interesting articles and links online."

"Ah, so you know me from top to bottom."

"No, not at all. You seem to defy categorization."

"Now *that* you read somewhere!"

"Yes," she giggles, "*le Monde*, I think!"

One thing leads to another and, when he glances back over his shoulder to the clock beside the bed, he realizes they've been on the phone for over an hour. And long ago they passed comfortably over that unsaid conversational road-bump that indicates they are now friends, not just acquaintances, and interested, hesitantly, in what comes next.

Late Monday morning, Kurt drives over to the old man's house. He's got a cold six pack of imported beer and a well-thumbed appointment calendar. Our man meets him on the front lawn and they head inside.

"I mean, I'm the devil pure and simple, I'm sure, but I have principles. So I think I should just tell you, one by one, the best stories of my daytime fucking of these bitches on my route."

It always takes our man a moment or two to adjust to Kurt's mode of prejudice. He just cannot believe the man is this callous or dismissive of other human beings who happen to be female and attracted to sex. After all, he has a teenage daughter he seems devoted to. What happens in his heart as he contemplates her welfare and happiness? This is all worthwhile material for something, but certainly not a romantic comedy. This is more like Louis-Ferdinand Celine, all the lights shot out and the cold as cold as can be.

Leading his friend inside, they find the old guy asleep before the television. Kurt, who is monitored during all working hours by the power company with a GPS device and an audio recorder attached to his shirt collar, has sent in a text to the head office that there is some problem at this address.

“Hey, old man, what’s the problem?” he recites dramatically for the benefit of his employers. Dad opens his eyes, sees his son with his childhood cohort, and smiles. Kurt continues his pantomime: “What did I tell you last time, you ornery son of a bitch? You can’t go messing with all these wires and the equipment without calling us first!” And then Kurt messes with the fuse box and wriggles some knobs on his diagnostic toolkit and effectively shoves Dad’s house off the grid for the time being.

As well as himself.

He turns back to the old man and offers him a fist

bump. Dad obliges, delighted. These days his off-the-charts laugh is just a wide grin and no noise whatsoever. Kurt has cracked the man up regularly since the boys were seven years old.

"Okay, my friend," the power company employee reassures him, "I've got to talk to the kid genius here for half an hour and we'll be back with regular programming before you can say Jack Robinson."

So these comparative youngsters huddle in the small back room behind the kitchen where our man has set up his desk. He takes the beer offered to him and opens his laptop.

"I've got long weekends," Kurt begins, "because I'm a senior employee. Free Friday through Sunday. Unless, of course, there's one of these increasingly popular ecology-ical disasters going on. Why don't we meet here each weekend and I'll tell you the whole thing. Should only take about a month."

Our man is a little overwhelmed. He was expecting this potentially interesting endeavor to manifest itself in the near or impossible-to-anticipate future, a nice idea best left to simmer on the back burner. But Kurt is a man on a mission. Our hero knows the tone, the long-range gaze, the almost religious commitment to a truth bound to meet with opposition.

"It's like that play you wrote," Kurt adds after swilling back some beer. "Those religious fanatics down in Texas. I read that. Bought the book from your website just to be a friend and supportive and all that." He looks away, pausing. "But that shit is real. Chicks wanting to get fucked by the preacher for god and the salvation of the world and all that. I mean, okay, this is a different thing. I'm not god and I don't even believe in god. But these bitches, once they start losing their girlish charms, they'll do anything, I mean anything. Find religion, for instance. And that's not the whole of it."

Kurt's eyes are wide, his face blank, holding his breath like a child before some impossible mistake he's just waiting to be punished for. "I mean, this is just to say that I feel for them." He leans back to drink but stops, insisting, "Really, I mean it." Finally, he does drink, reconsiders, and qualifies: "Well, okay, I feel for them sometimes. But it's like they'll go crazy. In fact, they do. They lose their minds." He presses the beer bottle against his forehead and gasps at the image of a dead-end life he can see through these housewives' eyes. "One, what's her name, she was valedictorian or some shit, she killed her kids and then herself!"

Our man remembers this.

"Veronica Steinman."

"Yeah, her. Fuck." Kurt stands and looks out the small window into the empty, blighted, backyards of the neighborhood. "Something's wrong out there."

Our man waits silently, watching, suspecting maybe his friend is suggesting something larger, or at least different, than a tell-all confession of his diabolical work-related sexual adventures.

Kurt turns back into the room, almost weak, unsteady.

"They're all a bunch of fucking degenerates," he decides, twisting off another cap and drinking.

"You mean the wives?"

"All of them," Kurt clarifies, sitting again. "The drunk over-weight husbands, the anorexic teenage daughters, the autistic computer geek sons. The whole parade. A whole civilization of retards. I get to see it all up close and personal, walking into these scumbags' homes and banging their wives who are on their third vodka and tonic by one in the afternoon, desperate to be fucked, to be felt up, to even just be spoken to like an attractive woman." He drinks and stares into the corner of the room. He suddenly looks old and afraid. "You see the thing is this," he manages to mumble before sitting forward, looking away, embarrassed. "The thing is I think I might feel sorry for them and…"

That seems to be as much as Kurt is willing to share

today. He remains there on the little old kitchen chair, staring down at the floor's cracked linoleum, gripping his beer, crying. Finally, as if to someone unseen, he whispers: "These bitches need me."

Ten minutes later, the power's back on and Kurt is on his way, drying his eyes. Dad's asleep again. Our hero offers his friend a clean handkerchief, makes a pot of coffee, and starts taking notes. Now he's got something to work with. Kurt's cynical sexual exploits are one thing. His outrageous misogyny another. The fact he is having some sort of quasi-spiritual mid-life crisis, a man who lives in a glorified toolshed in the backyard of the house he shares with his hated and estranged wife? That's another thing altogether. This is, he figures, primetime material. If he can get himself to reach down into the fetid bowels of contemporary culture's own disgust with itself and dredge up the requisite filth, he, even he, might be able to commit a genuine act of unapologetic commercial entertainment.

THREE

"But back at his desk in the city we find," our man sings Costello as he shoulders his way in through the door, "our trembling punch-drunken fighter…" He throws down his overnight bag, takes a gratifying pee in his own goddamn toilet and, for the moment, concedes to the capitalist scheme of things the rewards of private ownership. It's not yet ten in the morning on Tuesday and he has appointments throughout the day all over town. But first he'll make coffee and answer emails.

Reading again the message he has been composing for three weeks to the talented, lovely and famous actress in Brooklyn, he decides that what yesterday sounded sophisticated and even self-effacing today rings affected and stiff, too formal. So he starts all over again and gets right to the point: Saw your new film. You were great in it. I'm more anxious now than ever for you to like the script I sent you. Hope to hear from you soon. Yours, etcetera.

Good enough, he thinks and sends it off. This will lend him some moral heft at his two o'clock coffee meeting with his agent, Edward, who insists he doesn't make enough of an effort to be famous and influential. He changes into a fresh shirt and heads to the subway.

On the way, he passes the three hundred year old cemetery he often sits in to read and pauses to watch a man, a man a little older than himself, the groundskeeper, bundling up a clutch of fallen and broken branches, confident, knowledgeable, humble, at one with the materials he works with, from the twine, the shears, the brittle twigs he tosses into his wheelbarrow, the wheelbarrow itself, and his rake, his well-worn work gloves. As he moves off to other spaces of nature requiring his attention, this groundskeeper caresses the nearest tree like a brother. Our man discovers he's crying and reaches for his handkerchief.

There were no *Career Opportunity* titles in the station bookstore about how to become a groundskeeper. But, right now, it's all he wants to be: to tend, to neaten, to protect, to be subject to the weather, to have his hands calloused with honest labor, to be able to look out at the end of the day to a swath of the world well managed, to be justifiably fatigued as opposed to just aggravated and beat. He remembers reading about Islam in his youth, discovering the word meant submission, and that this submission entailed a stewardship of nature, a responsibility to assist and protect, to nurture. As he descends into the garbage strewn, urine-soaked subway he feels small. What has he done with his life? Is the talented, lovely and famous actress in Brooklyn really essential? Does he need to continue this mad race for last place in the estimation of the entertainment business? How long would he be interested in manufacturing sexy little USB thumb drives anyway?

He stands at the floor-to-ceiling window looking down at midtown traffic listening as his lawyer, Emily, a sharp-witted fifty-year-old woman, explains some interesting details of being a responsible grownup citizen.

"Simply stated, a last Will and Testament is a legal document that lets you designate individuals or charities to receive your property and possessions when you pass away. These individuals and charities are referred to as beneficiaries."

"Okay. So far so good."

"A Last Will also allows you, for instance," she continues, busy with her emails, "to name a guardian to care for your underage children."

"I have no children."

"That you know of."

Piqued, our man turns in from the view and watches his friend of many years multitask.

"What are you trying to say?"

Emily dispatches an email, closes her laptop, slides it aside and removes her reading glasses.

"Only that one needs to be careful. You weren't always the quiet and unassuming elder statesman of American romantic comedy, kiddo. I recall a lot of broken hearts. Just have to make sure there are no skeletons in the closets, no disgruntled scion loitering in the halls of justice."

"Wow," he mumbles, feeling this new intelligence like a punch in the chest. He crosses the spacious corporate calm and sits on the attractive modernist couch. "Why even make stories up at all? Life itself is so rife with contention."

"Tell me about it. There'd be nothing for us lawyers to do otherwise." But seeing her old friend and associate's winded incomprehension, she stands and comes around the front of her desk with a little less professional exactitude. "Listen, the main purpose of a Will is to ensure that your wishes, and not the default laws of the state, will be followed upon your death."

"How do we begin?

"The paperwork is pretty standard. I can get started on that. You, meanwhile, need to go home and make a list of your possessions, property, and the individuals or charities you would like to leave them to when you die. You still married?"

"No."

"Formally divorced?"

"I paid the state what they said they were owed and I have the receipt to prove it."

"How is she?"

"Clara?"

"I so liked her. How could you blow that?"

He's fond of Emily but she can sometimes be like a bossy little sister and, though he resists, frustrated, he gives in and defends himself clumsily.

"We were young. We were in love. We changed."

"You still dating the fashion model," she asks casually as she returns to her desk, dons her glasses and resumes shuffling papers. And now he's sure he's hearing the faint echo of a long-lost minor resentment. There was, after all, that evening in Rome twenty years ago, hip to hip in the backseat of the car returning to the hotel after completing the film. She was a junior associate at the firm, just out of law school. He caressed her bare leg, she rested her head on his shoulder. Then her boss called demanding facts and figures. They never mentioned it again.

But now, concerning the fashion model, the Mistress: Is he still dating her?

"Maybe," he allows. "I don't know."

"And what are her expectations?"

"Her expectations of what?"

"Listen, wise guy, she's married. She's married to and has children with a seemingly wealthy real estate developer who's recently been indicted on however many counts of fraud and who will most likely be in prison or flee the country before the end of the year. What will be the nature of your relationship then?"

The more Emily speaks the more reality comes to resemble a dense tangle of thorny branches through which he must struggle to see passing traffic.

"Holy shit."

"My feelings exactly. Has she got financial resources of her own from her long and illustrious career?"

"No, I think that's all used up."

"So she and her children could be destitute when this creep goes to jail?"

"Well, it's hard to imagine but I mean…"

"Will she depend on you then?"

"What, I… What have I got to…? A small apartment in

Nowheresville, Manhattan, a lot of books, about a hundred grand in an annuity somewhere."

"It's not all about cash money, you know. Most importantly, of course, are the rights in your movies which can generate income in perpetuity. Intellectual Property. Those rights can be left to your designated beneficiaries. Clara? The fashion model? Both? Neither? All or just some? None at all? The potential for heartbreak and scandal is, of course, endless."

"She does have a name, you know."

"Look," Emily says, standing, "over all these years of ceaseless productivity you've generated a list of material and intellectual assets people might want to fight over later."

Breathless, he sits back and accepts the inevitable:

"I apologize."

"Don't get dramatic on me." She smiles, coming across the carpet to sit on the couch beside him. "Here's a list of things you need to address." He studies a cheat sheet of items to tick off before one puts one's shoulder to the wheel and trudges on towards the great beyond in earnest. "Go home and think about it."

Walking wistfully down Seventh Avenue towards Chelsea he understands he is in fact no longer dating the fashion model. After their high-speed tumble in the back of the taxi and another hour of a quieter passion safely inside his apartment, the Mistress announced a new chapter in her life.

"Spain," our man repeated, on his back, his gaze drifting through the shadows on the ceiling, surprised but not exactly hurt. "You're moving to Spain?"

"For Antonio."

Antonio was a hugely successful photographer of rock stars in the nineteen-eighties who made the Mistress' career happen with a perfume advertisement when she was thirteen. In his seventies now, the man is bravely battling sobriety and writing his memoirs in a mansion outside Madrid.

"He needs me now," she sighed with some emotion.

Our man stops on the sidewalk to wait for the light and realizes he's relieved, though it's not a comforting sensation. He'll miss her, of course, and not just for the uncomplicated sex and associated hilarity. It's her common sense and lack of sentimentality he'll pine for, the clearheaded gut instinct that is so much a breath of fresh air, that tug on his back pocket to warn him of saying too much, of venturing too far, of his reckless belief in the reasonableness of people everywhere. He's had occasion to note she's a warm-hearted cynic. But she knows what's hers and assumes her responsibilities with the earnestness of an assassin while remaining at all times perfectly generous and gracious.

“I don’t like sharing,” she once confided in him. “If someone needs my coat, I will give it to him. But I will not share it.”

He suspects something of this lies behind her decision to flee the husband with her daughters and take up refuge in the mansion outside Madrid. The husband once needed her own small fortune for speculative ends that came to nothing. She gave it freely at the time, lost it all, and refuses now to share in his demise.

So be it. Drama, prime time style. Subtitled.

Ah! But what could have been!

Still, he shudders to think of it. What if she had looked to him, our protagonist, for sanctuary, for something more like a stable relationship, with two little girls in tow?

Impossible. Unthinkable. And, of course, she saw this with the unerring precision of a dedicated mom and not just the instinct of a seasoned debauchee. Our hero might have been fun, of course. He doubted she’d deny this. For one thing there were all those events he was invited to which provided an opportunity for her to wear some unique piece of *haute couture* from her own wardrobe that had not been seen anywhere in a decade. But, too, he was definitely helpful in smaller matters as she, in her early forties, concerned herself with her daughters' education. He'd lie in bed afterward, tangled in the sheets watching her peruse his bookshelves in the nude. She'd recently read an article about the Great Books curriculum. Pulling a tome down and flipping through it, she displayed it for him: "Plato. Do you think the girls should read this?"

"Not at nine years old."

So he's relieved in the particular. The Mistress should go to Antonio, live large, be an inspiration for an old man's last years because she enjoys that sort of thing and, meanwhile, get her girls educated. But he's troubled generally, recognizing once again a recurring motif: Why has he spent so much of his fifty-three years alone? As his lawyer so pointedly asked about Clara: How could he blow that?

Clara, his wife of ten years, had been like a guardian angel appearing before him at a point of probable disaster; success, fame, money, untethered sexual curiosity and plenty of opportunity to indulge. But he was beat, spiritually exhausted and divided, more than willing to forsake the whole parade, the career, the acquired good regard along with truckloads of its opposite. Clara materialized, graceful, soulful, mysterious in the simplicity of her needs, becoming the inspiration for changing his ways and disregarding the supposed importance of the battlefield squalor commonly called show business. He discovered a tenderness in himself he never thought possible, redoubled his efforts to make good work, or not, but always with the aim of protecting her and fighting his way to a reasonable exit leading to some imagined place of peace, quiet, reconciliation, and…

He's on a different street corner. The sun is setting. How long has he been there? An older Black man who seems associated with a delivery van idling at the curb is watching, concerned.

"Was I talking out loud to myself?"

"I guess so."

"Sorry."

"No problem, man. It'll all work out."

"You shouldn't even be doing your own accounting and legal," Edward insists petulantly. He's our man's agent, though he has never actually done anything for him in that regard.

"It's not all that hard," our hero shrugs. "Of course it is boring. But it's idiotic to spend four hundred dollars an hour on accountants and such."

Edward shakes with impatience and fishes in his pocket for his credit card to pay for their coffees.

"And if you are going to piss away an hour and a half of your day before supper you should be outlining a story people are going to be interested in!"

"People were interested in the Gaddis series idea. I mean it was optioned, right?"

"Of course, until they discovered you planned to adapt an 800-page novel made up entirely of unattributed dialogue into a thirty-six-episode limited series that amounts to a total take-down of American free enterprise culture."

"Right? It was hilarious. No hard feelings. They chickened out, though."

"They didn't chicken out! They're responsible American capitalists insulted by the accurate portrayal of their greed and childish violence!"

"Well maybe. Sure. They were honest about that, I have to say. But to return to our earlier standoff: Substance abuse has a long and profitable heritage. Common human failings. You know, good people gone wrong, redemption, betrayal, weakness. That kind of thing."

"Alcoholism, drug abuse, it's all been done. Sex addiction is where it's at now."

"Yeah?"

"Please."

"I'm not kidding. Really? Sex addiction?"

"This is what I mean! This is what happens to a person

who doesn't engage in social media. You're out of touch."

"But sex addiction is a thing?"

"A major thing. They have twelve-step programs. It's totally legitimate."

"But it's real?"

"What do you mean is it real? It's advertised!"

"No, I mean. Forget what I mean. Listen, I have this story idea for a series about a suburban power company meter-reader and his relationships with all these dissatisfied housewives whose homes he needs to enter during the day."

"And he's a sex addict?"

"No, but maybe some of the housewives are."

"No, that won't fly these days. The man has to be the sex addict, especially if he's White and entitled."

"Well, the guy I have in mind is not exactly entitled but he is White. But that can change, depending."

"Depending on what?"

"Financing of course! Edward, I'm trying to be a team player here! Focus!"

"I like this new opportunism you're embracing. Positive. Let's go."

Out on the sidewalk Edward can barely contain himself, trembling with the prospect of success that might be passing them by unseen and, so, feverishly scrolling through his text messages to make sure. “What are you reading, for instance?”

“You won’t be pleased.”

“Of course I won’t. But I know you’re not reading best sellers, online life-style guides, the trade papers, or doing anything so common as tweeting.”

“That’s true.”

Edward refuses to respond. Instead, he scans the area for a cab.

Our man is really more exhausted than flippant, not wishing to ridicule his agent’s confidently held, superficial, and temporary convictions, knowing as he does that these are, in fact, the tools of the younger man’s trade. But he goes on and answers honestly. “Melville.”

“Current?”

“Still read but dead since 1891.”

“Period. Okay. There’s interest in that now. Was this Melville successful?”

“No not really in his lifetime but I think this meter-reader idea is important.”

“Is the meter-reader thing related to Melville?”

“No but of course all great stories are related to other great stories.”

“Speak English.”

“There are some very influential writers who were not

successful in a popular sense but whose achievements propel a lot of what we read and see in the mainstream anyhow."

"Are you making this shit up just to annoy me?"

"No, it's my friend, this writer Aldo, he's got this whole theory."

"Fuck off," Edward concedes congenially, shaking hands before ducking into a taxi. "Text me when you hear from our lovely and talented movie star in Brooklyn. And we should talk about this depraved meter-reader thing and whoever the fuck this Melville is."

The subject of our inquiry wanders further east, leisurely, to what he fondly refers to as his other office, a less than swank but happening French Moroccan bistro on Sixth Avenue where he holds most of his meetings. Arriving fifteen minutes early for his rendezvous with the Girl of the Glove, Muriel, he sits at the bar and orders a Sauvignon Blanc with a small dish of sautéed spinach and enjoys the bartender's back. She's an athletically svelte Asian American girl in her thirties and he's seen her here before. She usually sexes herself up tastefully to work the evening bar crowd. But this afternoon she's wearing just black jeans and a black sports bra under a snug fitting black lace see-through blouse. It's a nice, casual, friendly assault on the senses and, for reasons he's never understood, he tries not to get caught appreciating the effect.

At exactly three o'clock, his mobile bleeps and he assumes it's the girl saying she'll be late. He hates this nonsense. Since the popular use of mobile devices no one is ever on time, as if calling at the last minute to say you'll be late is not in fact being late. Or maybe she's texting to cancel. And suddenly he's weak in arm and leg.

But he's surprised. It's Muriel saying she's at a table opposite the bar. Swiveling around on his stool, there she is, seated at one of the small zinc-topped tables twelve or thirteen feet away. He steps over and sits beside her on the narrow banquette. They shake hands.

"Nice to meet you," he says.

"Likewise," she replies with a shy but devious grin.

He sees her gloves laid aside on the table, neatly placed and aligned, as if in prayer.

"There they are, together again."

"At last."

He is grateful the bartender stops by just then and asks what they would like because he believes he was about to ask Muriel if she had, the previous Saturday, deliberately left her glove behind for him to retrieve. In the time it takes to order a glass of wine he understands what a bad start that might have been to whatever it is he suspects is being initiated here: friendship, romance, scandal? Unfortunately for those of us eager to see our man confirmed as a voluptuary, a predator, a wrecker of youth, Muriel surgically unplugs any immediate prospects:

"My boyfriend might join us a little later if that's okay."

Crushed and grateful simultaneously, wondering fleetingly if this is all just a young woman's chop at the ankles of an established man who seems to dig her, but putting a brave face on it, our hero slips out of his coat and smiles venerably.

"Of course. Are you at school together?"

"He's actually in the graduate program studying theater. He told me all about your work. He'd love to meet you."

And, so, with that settled, they wile away the late afternoon and he finds it easy, freed from previous expectations, to be himself with her. Though their experiences are very different they respond to the same kinds of things. She's never read Henry Miller, for instance, but she knows the *Diaries* of Anaïs Nin by heart.

"And you've never felt like reading Miller? I mean, she writes about him a lot in the diaries."

"Yes, I know, but I guess he seemed to me like just another one of these helpless men in her life." She sips her wine and attenuates: "Though, I admit, it was a while ago. I read her diaries when I was, like, fifteen. The first four volumes anyway."

"Really? Fifteen?"

"Some of it did go over my head," she admits sensibly.

He rarely has the pleasure of conversing so freely, of referencing as widely and casually about his reading. She loves Melville! She's curious about Lispector! She's reading Hannah Arendt in a course at school! As she said on the phone, she is certainly the child of academics and is comfortably intellectual. But she's also used to being watched and admired like any attractive young woman and seems to enjoy toying with it within reason. Which makes him ask himself if she is, just now, being brave or reckless. Either way, she is confident. That's clear. And that seems to take the heat off him. He allows her to drive whatever it is they're both riding along on. She is not innocent of her charms.

"I wonder," he muses, sliding down in the banquette, signaling for another glass of wine.

"You wonder what?" she asks, leaning closer, grinning, her hand finding his where it lies on the seat of the banquette. If this is not flirting or, as a lawyer might say, chaste amorous relations, he does not know what is. Looking down at her fingers he answers:

"I wonder how much, if anything, did go over your head at fifteen."

This gives her pause. The mischievous intimacy of a moment ago is dispelled. She sits up, looks away at nothing, and reconsiders as she traces the tip of her finger lightly along beneath her chin.

"I don't believe the sex made much of an impression, for instance. I was drawn into all that running around Paris and trying to write. The grappling with conscience! The fascinating friends who were also so frustrating! I was a brainy little brat, honest. The houseboat! I used to day-dream I had a houseboat too!"

"You know, of course, she invented a lot of this stuff, right?"

Muriel is brought up hard by this. She tilts her head a little to the side, and studies our man's face closely, her pretty jaw slack and her lower lip thrust forward.

"No."

"It's true. I mean, I think the writing is great, the in-sights, the reflections, the prose, the whole thing. I reread sections all the time. But I consider it a novel."

"She made it up?"

"She started from real experience and reworked it over the years. She really should have just called it a novel, I think. Miller suggested that too."

Now Muriel is getting suspicious, maybe he's trying to play with her. "I don't believe it," she declares imperiously and sips her wine.

"Well, it is all pretty controversial. You should read, oh, what's it called? There's a biography, the author's name escapes me. It caused quite a ruckus when it came out back in the nineties."

She sits back and sighs.

"Okay, change of subject. I'm not emotionally prepared for all this. How did you spend your night?"

"You mean after I spoke with you on the phone?"

"You said you weren't sleepy."

How did he spend his night? Most likely he paced his childhood room eagerly anticipating this very rendezvous while listening to make sure his dad wasn't risking his life heading down the hall to the bathroom on his own. But then he remembers wearing himself out and, sleep not being an option…

"I stayed up late and watched a movie."

"What was it? Hurry, I'm still not over the shock of Anaïs Nin's alleged duplicity!"

He laughs and wants to touch her somehow, to just reach out and claim a physical intimacy they can try and sort out later. But he stops himself.

"*Harry & Tonto*, with Art Carney, early seventies."

"What's it about?"

"Old people."

“Wasn’t Tonto a famous Indian or something?”

“A famous native American character in the classic *Lone Ranger* adventure series.”

“Also early seventies?”

“No, much earlier. Long story. In this movie Tonto is a cat.”

“And who’s Harry?”

“The old man who owns the cat. Art Carney. Ever heard of *The Honeymooners*?”

“No.”

“Okay, my friend, I think we’ve reached the outer limits of our mutually acknowledged formative influences.”

With a frown, she leans into him, shoulder to shoulder, and seems about to expire.

“But the *Outer Limits* was a show, right?”

He takes her hand where it lies beaten and limp on her knee and gives it a fortifying squeeze. This seems to be all she’s ever wanted, a sign she can now let the whole of her light pleasing frame rest against him fully. Our subject glances over to catch the eye of the bartender who, though doing her best to ignore the finer points of this charming comedy, now tilts her head and gestures to their nearly empty glasses and mimes, “two more?”

He nods back, yes, two more will be just the ticket. And the girl needs to eat so he orders the sautéed spinach and the hummus plate. He's now convinced the boyfriend was an invention to protect herself in the early stages of perilous flirtation with this quiet but rascally older guy. But then the boyfriend is standing right there beside them.

"Oh, hi," Muriel says, untroubled, looking up through her long dark lashes past our hero to an impossibly handsome and earnest young man with a backpack.

At twenty-seven, David knows our hero's movies like the back of his own hand, speaks intelligently about them, and isn't fawning. On fire with creative ambition of his own, the young man has a radically personal impetus to his overall creative project which our man can't help admiring, though he worries for the guy.

"I just want to take apart this body of work, Chekhov, which on the face of things means nothing to me. I mean it's a big effort for me to learn why these things he's got characters discussing are so important."

"This is not me," our man begins, "I'm quoting, though I don't know who. But 'the effort to understand a foreigner is the height of our articulation.' Something like that."

"I'll write that down," Muriel says and starts typing it into her laptop. The bartender buys them all a round.

"Yeah, I'm just trying to understand but letting that, I don't know, that uncertainty be part of the drama. You know what I mean?"

"It becomes an effort of history, an act of historical thinking, even apart from a creative strategy. But they're related."

"Yeah. I admit my ignorance as the foundation of my creative process."

"As long as you make the effort to form meaning out of it."

"Of course."

"You don't want to make sketch-comedy waxing hilarious about your ignorance of Chekhov."

"Yes! No! Not that! Thank you! It's the effort to understand something so distant from our popular anticipations that I want to, in a way, I guess, enact. There's meaning in that. Right?"

Our man hasn't had such attention-sharpening fun in months. He likes the open-minded desperation with which this kid is hammering together chunks of useful intelligence, split-second inspiration, theory and practical knowhow from wherever the hell he's been able to grab it, from pop songs, TV shows, subway advertisements. He thinks the kid's a doer. If he sometimes has to sound like an idiot, so be it. Join the club. They exchange emails and phone numbers. He's got books at his place this young man needs access to.

Before long, Muriel allows herself to be a quiet and studious observer, elbows on the small table, intense, happy and concentrated, whom both the older and younger man cast glances at for confirmation, objective proof that they are not talking nonsense. Or maybe they're just showing off. She remains, however, a sphinx, seated beside our man on the banquette as her boyfriend sits across from them. Our man studies David studying Muriel, her expressions, her movements, her attention. The younger man cares for her approbation and feels acutely that she is parsimonious with it. But the older man, decades ahead in the exercise of self-doubt, is sure she's just exercising the wisdom of reticence. She won't speak unless she knows what she wants to say. And, in the meantime, she will assess what she hears from others.

Time passes. It's dark outside.

"But how did you come up with an idea like that," David asks, referring to a scene in a film our man made a decade ago.

"David," Muriel interjects, "stop interrogating him. And look, it's almost six-thirty. We have to get to the theater."

Muriel is interning on David's new staging of *The Cherry Orchard*, a play our man sat through thirty years ago in the pathetically unlikely hope of sleeping with an actress friend and which, even now, makes him sleepy just to remember.

"Do you have a role," he asks Muriel.

"No!" she exclaims with a small unconvinced laugh of relief. "I'm just taking notes. And I run errands. I get three humanities credits." But the relevance of the question still hangs in the air. She is aware of her beauty and poise right now in a way that displeases. She'd like their attention to move on to others things and busies herself with objects in her satchel. Our man turns away and looks at his knee to give her space. But David leans in close to him and asks with the humble curiosity of the hardworking aspirant:

"She should be in the movies, right?"

Muriel rolls her eyes to the ceiling with a barely concealed sigh before heading off to the lady's room. Letting her get far enough away, our man finally answers:

"Or a novel."

He watches this smart, endearing, and probably impermanent young couple hurry away east across 13th Street, repeatedly turning to wave goodbye before disappearing into the noisy darkness and the glare of headlights. "New friends," he admits half aloud to himself as his cell phone trembles and bleeps. He fishes it out of his pocket and answers. "Hey, it's me."

www.ingramcontent.com/pod-product-compliance
Lightning Source LLC
Chambersburg PA
CBHW060538310726
48982CB00009B/1295/J

* 9 7 8 1 7 3 7 9 2 7 4 4 0 *